Jeanie & Genie

THE FIRST WISH

 BY **TRISH GRANTED**
ILLUSTRATED BY **MANUELA LÓPEZ**

LITTLE SIMON
New York   London   Toronto   Sydney   New Delhi

 **LITTLE SIMON**

An imprint of Simon & Schuster Children's Publishing Division · 1230 Avenue of the Americas, New York, New York 10020 · First Little Simon paperback edition January 2021

Copyright © 2021 by Simon & Schuster, Inc.

All rights reserved, including the right of reproduction in whole or in part in any form.

LITTLE SIMON is a registered trademark of Simon & Schuster, Inc., and associated colophon is a trademark of Simon & Schuster, Inc.

For information about special discounts for bulk purchases, please contact Simon & Schuster Special Sales at 1-866-506-1949 or business@simonandschuster.com.

The Simon & Schuster Speakers Bureau can bring authors to your live event.

For more information or to book an event contact the Simon & Schuster Speakers Bureau at 1-866-248-3049 or visit our website at www.simonspeakers.com.

Designed by Brittany Fetcho

Manufactured in the United States of America 1120 MTN

10 9 8 7 6 5 4 3 2 1

Cataloging-in-Publication Data for this title is available from the Library of Congress.

ISBN 978-1-5344-7466-6 (hc)

ISBN 978-1-5344-7465-9 (pbk)

ISBN 978-1-5344-7467-3 (eBook)

TABLE OF CONTENTS

WEIRD WEDNESDAY

Wednesdays in Jeanie Bell's second-grade classroom were predictable.

And that's just how Jeanie Bell liked them.

Ms. Patel always started the day with journal writing. In her journal, Jeanie had written about the new trick her dog, Bear, had learned at breakfast that morning.

She'd done her science work ahead of time. Labeling plant parts was easy-peasy.

But Jeanie *couldn't* work ahead in gym. Luckily, on Wednesdays the class did yoga. Tree pose was perfect for resting . . . but also for practicing for the spelling bee. Plus, yoga meant she didn't have to worry about fending off the Lee triplets in dodgeball!

At lunch Jeanie ate while she read a few chapters of the book she'd chosen for independent reading. She didn't want to lose her lead in Ms. Patel's Reading Challenge.

All in all, it was a totally normal Wednesday.

But when Jeanie returned to room 2B after lunch, something *un*predictable and *not* normal was happening.

A girl Jeanie didn't recognize stood at the front of the class.

Ms. Patel clapped her hands twice to get everyone's attention. "Class, this is Willow Davis," she said. "Today is her first day at Rivertown Elementary."

Jeanie wouldn't want to be the new kid in class. She hated being the center of attention.

But this girl didn't seem to mind the attention! She wore a big smile and a bracelet with little bells that jingled as she waved to the class.

Ms. Patel asked Willow to tell everyone about herself.

"My house has a wishing well," Willow began. "I love shooting stars and blowing out birthday candles. And I like to draw—especially ladybugs."

"That's lovely. And where are you from, Willow?" asked Ms. Patel.

Willow hesitated. "Um . . . all over, I guess."

Ms. Patel smiled. "You can take the empty seat in the second row," she said.

Willow practically floated toward her new desk . . . which was right behind Jeanie's.

Willow tapped Jeanie on the back. "What's your name?"

Jeanie raised her eyebrows. Ms. Patel was beginning a math lesson on fractions. Jeanie knew she should be paying attention. But she didn't want to be rude. "I'm Jeanie," she replied, then quickly turned back toward the front of the room.

"What's your favorite color?" Willow asked. "Mine's rainbow."

"It's green," Jeanie whispered.

"What subject do you like best?" asked Willow.

Has this girl never been to school before?! Jeanie wondered.

"Math," murmured Jeanie, hoping Willow would take the hint.

Ms. Patel was comparing fractions to slices of pie. Each slice was one quarter of the pie. Jeanie tried to focus. But another pesky question came from over her shoulder.

"Do you believe in magic? I do!"
Willow's eyes sparkled, and a dreamy
look spread across her face.

Jeanie did not believe in magic.
She believed in paying attention.
And facts and math and fractions.

Willow was friendly, but she was also at least *a fraction* annoying. And her questions were still coming.

"What did you wish for on your last birthday?" asked Willow.

Jeanie sighed. At the moment, she *wished* Willow would just stop talking.

Chapter 2

WILLOW'S FIRST DAY

When the last bell of the day rang, Willow watched her new classmates gather their belongings.

The Lee triplets had basketball practice. Aaron and Ben pretended to shoot hoops while Charlie frantically searched for his sneakers. Then they all bolted out of the room. Nico Romero and Zora Klein argued about whose turn it was to take Jelly Bean, the class hamster, home for the night.

And a girl named Jeanie Bell carefully checked her homework folder, waved to Willow, and headed out the door.

Willow looked around the empty room. Classroom 2B had a reading nook bursting with books, a bulletin board on the history of Rivertown, and a giant word wall that described Willow's first day of real school pretty perfectly: "exciting," "strange," and "new."

Plus, Willow's desk was next to the window, where a pair of orange butterflies had spent the afternoon playing tag.

It was also next to Jeanie Bell. Willow liked how Jeanie had lined up her pencils so perfectly. Willow's desk, on the other hand, was already a jumble of strawberry-scented erasers and fairy doodles.

But the best part of the day had been art class. The teacher was a funny man with a funny mustache, named Mr. Bloom. He had shown everyone how to make collages out of found objects.

Willow used the most fantastic things she could find: glittery buttons, feathers, and gum wrappers.

"What is it?" asked Jeanie when she saw Willow's creation.

"A flying kittycorn, of course. She's part kitten, part bird, part unicorn, and *all* amazing," Willow said.

"Cool!" said Jeanie. "I never would have thought of making up a creature like a kittycorn."

Willow smiled. She wondered if Jeanie was up for a joke. "What's the difference between a unicorn and a carrot?" she asked.

Jeanie shrugged.

"One is a funny beast, and the other is a bunny feast!" Willow cried. It was one of her best jokes . . . but would Jeanie think so?

Jeanie stared at Willow. Then she started laughing. That made Willow

laugh too. Then they both laughed even harder.

Willow was pretty sure art class was going to be her favorite thing about Rivertown Elementary.

But now, it was time to go home.

And in the blink of an eye, Willow

was walking through her front door. The sound of wind chimes announced her arrival.

She dropped her backpack in the hall, grabbed a cookie from the kitchen, and headed for her mother's office.

"Mom!" Willow called as she barged inside. "Are you ready to hear about my first day of school?

Art class was awesome, and I think I made a new best friend, and—"

"Hi, honey," Willow's mom interrupted. "I want to hear all about your first day, but I need to check tomorrow's forecast and star alignment, and make sure all our schedules are on track. Can this wait?"

"Sure," said Willow as she touched the necklace she always wore. "Now that we've moved to Rivertown, I've got plenty of work to do."

Willow's mother looked up from her calendar and said with a knowing smile, "I'm sure you do."

Chapter 3

MAKING FRIENDS

The next morning at breakfast, Jeanie told her family about her new classmate.

"Willow is funny and super artsy," said Jeanie. "But she talks a LOT!"

Jeanie tore four squares of waffle from her plate and fed them to Bear. He gobbled them down and barked for more. *Arf! Arf! Arf!*

29

"Bear talks a lot," Jeanie's little brother, Jake, pointed out. "And you like *him*. . . ."

Jeanie rolled her eyes.

"It sounds like Willow's just trying to make friends," said Jeanie's mom. "It's hard to be new."

Jeanie's dad nodded. "Just be your sweet, sunny self. I bet you'll find you have things in common," he said.

Jeanie knew her parents were right. If she was going to sit next to Willow all year, it would be better to get along. Being nice was the practical thing to do. And if there was anything Jeanie was . . . it was practical.

At school later that morning, Jeanie tried to be friendly.

"How do you like Rivertown so far?" she asked Willow.

"I love it!" Willow gushed. "The shops downtown are so cute. And I can't wait to throw a penny in that fountain in front of Gio's Pizza. Something about this town just feels . . . special."

Ms. Patel called the class to order. Then she began their science lesson.

"Have you been to Rivertown Gardens?" asked Willow. "I want to see the exotic flowers!"

"Not yet," Jeanie whispered. "I like ice-skating better. Glimmer Pond is really pretty in the winter."

"Jeanie," called Ms. Patel. "What did we just learn about why plants need the sun to grow?"

Jeanie's stomach clenched. "I'm n-n-not sure . . . ," she stammered.

"Please pay attention," Ms. Patel scolded. "I won't ask again."

Jeanie's cheeks burned. She hated getting in trouble. And it was all Willow's fault! From now on, Jeanie's lips would stay zipped.

When lunchtime came, Jeanie grabbed her book and found a quiet corner of the cafeteria.

But then she spotted Willow sitting all alone. Jeanie remembered what her parents had said about being new.

So she took the seat next to Willow instead.

"I'm sorry about this morning," said Willow.

"That's okay," said Jeanie. "We're not supposed to talk in class. But maybe we can go to Rivertown Gardens together sometime."

Willow's eyes lit up. "I'll ask my mom!" She glanced at Jeanie's book. "What are you reading?" she asked.

"It's an awesome series about a time-traveling mouse," Jeanie answered. "You can borrow the first book if you want."

When Willow leaned forward to get a better look, Jeanie noticed something shiny glinting at her neck.

It was a pretty gold chain with a charm that looked like a teapot. Or was it an elephant head? Jeanie wasn't sure.

"I like your necklace," said Jeanie.

"Um, thanks," said Willow. She quickly tucked the charm back inside her shirt. "These books sound great!"

Jeanie smiled. Maybe her dad was right. Maybe she and Willow had more in common than she'd thought.

GRAND TOUR

Lunch period went by in a flash.

Willow swallowed her last bite of meatloaf. "I definitely need to start bringing my lunch," she said. "This meatloaf reminds me of when I made pumpkin pie and forgot the sugar."

Jeanie laughed. "Come on, I'll show you around on the way back to class."

Willow dumped her tray, then followed Jeanie into the hallway.

They passed by a classroom filled with the slightly off-tune sounds of the pre-K music class. Willow spotted one tiny boy struggling to ding his triangle at the right moment.

The fifth-grade hallway was even louder.

"That's the water fountain where the Show-Off Showdown happened," said Jeanie. "The choir kids and the theater kids both wanted to do morning announcements. They settled it with a sing-off."

"I guess they just had to *du-et*," Willow joked.

Jeanie pointed out the auditorium and the principal's office. Then she stopped in front of the library.

When Willow peeked inside, she saw shelves bursting with books, beanbag chairs, and computer stations. Murals of some of her favorite stories covered the walls. Willow could almost picture fairy godmothers and fire-breathing dragons flying around the room!

"I would love to spend more time here," Jeanie said. "There are *so* many books I haven't read yet. But we usually only come once a week."

Willow nodded. She would have to keep that in mind if she checked out any books. Sometimes she had

trouble remembering to return them!
Next they turned down a hall with
windows that overlooked a baseball
diamond, track, and meadow where a
soccer game was going on.

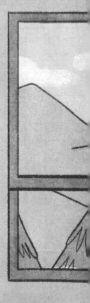

"Those are the sports fields," said Jeanie. "Someone else might have to show them to you, though. I'm not exactly a star athlete."

"Me neither," said Willow as she watched a soccer player flick the ball into the net for a goal. "At least, I don't *think* I am. I've never really played sports before."

Jeanie shifted from one foot to the other. "I try," she said. "But I'm just not that good. Or fast. Or strong."

"But you're smart," said Willow. "This is only my second day, and I can already tell."

Jeanie shrugged. "I don't need to be an Olympian or anything," she said. "I just wish I was a little better at *one* sport."

Willow could hear the longing in Jeanie's voice. She reached for her necklace. Then she stopped. She wasn't sure if the time was right.

Keeping her eyes on the field, Willow said, "Well, we have PE next, so at least we can both be terrible together."

Jeanie smiled and said, "Yeah! But remember—we can't talk during class."

Willow nodded, then pretended to lock her lips and throw away the invisible key.

That made Jeanie giggle, and suddenly Willow realized she was really happy at Rivertown Elementary. It was a nice, normal, totally average school.

And things that were *nice*, *normal*, and *average* were always ready for a little magic....

Chapter 5

GAME TIME

The class walked single file into the gym.

Jeanie watched Willow. She had such a bounce in her step! Jeanie wished she could feel that excited about PE. But she'd much rather be in the library, curled up with a good book or doing homework.

When they'd all lined up in two neat rows, their PE teacher,

Ms. Martinez, blew her whistle.

"It's dodgeball day!" she announced.

Jeanie groaned. Dodgeball was her least favorite sport. The Lee triplets threw the balls so fast Jeanie could barely keep track. And she was never quick enough to get out of the way!

While Ms. Martinez explained the rules of the game, Jeanie's tummy began to feel shaky. Her heart beat faster, too. Jeanie broke her no-talking-in-class rule.

She turned to Willow and whispered, "I wish we weren't playing dodgeball!"

For a moment Willow closed her eyes, like she was trying to decide what to say. She was twirling her pretty necklace in her hands.

Then something strange happened. Jeanie thought she saw a golden flash.

"And finally, the most important rule of dodgeball is never, ever . . . well . . . um." Ms. Martinez paused as her face went totally blank. "Actually . . . I'm not sure what it is."

Jeanie had never seen the PE teacher so confused. What was going on?

"Class, I've made a mistake," continued Ms. Martinez. "Today isn't dodgeball day. It's broomball day!"

Jeanie's eyebrows shot up. She didn't love broomball, but it was *way* better than getting pelted by the Lee triplets.

Everyone marched over to the equipment closet to grab brooms, nets, and a ball.

"Can you believe it?" Jeanie asked Willow.

"Um, no," Willow said, "I can't. I guess Ms. Martinez just, um, changed her mind totally on her own by herself."

Jeanie noticed Willow's cheeks were a little pink. And they hadn't even started playing.

Ms. Martinez blew her whistle again. "Jeanie, Willow, you're both on the blue team."

The girls walked over to join their classmates. The Lee triplets were already smacking the ball around.

"At least we're teammates," said Willow.

Jeanie took a deep breath and put on a blue jersey. "Let's do this!" she said.

The girls clinked brooms and headed to one side of the gym.

Ready or not, it was time to play ball.

Chapter 6

RAIN, RAIN, GO AWAY

"That actually wasn't so bad," Willow told Jeanie as they headed back to classroom 2B.

In fact, Willow had sort of enjoyed the game. She hadn't scored a goal, but she'd had a few good shots. And she'd spent the whole time pretending to be a witch riding a broom!

At first, Jeanie had told Willow she looked silly. But soon both girls

were racing around and cackling loudly.

For quiet reading time, Jeanie chose books about magical creatures. She told Willow she liked reading about fantasy worlds!

Willow was really curious to learn more, but she didn't want to get

Jeanie in trouble. Willow decided to wait until later to ask.

Before they knew it, it was time for afternoon recess. Gray storm clouds were gathering in the sky as they filed out onto the playground.

"What do you like to do during recess?" Willow asked Jeanie.

"I usually sit over there and read by myself," said Jeanie, pointing to a big, leafy oak tree. Willow considered that. It wasn't exactly something they could do together.

"We could make up a dance routine!" suggested Willow. "Or go on a treasure hunt. Or do cartwheels."

Jeanie blushed. "I can't really do a cartwheel."

"I'll show you," said Willow. "Just make sure your hands are even, like this!"

Willow sprang forward, circling the playground as the wind picked up.

"I'm a twisting tornado!" she shouted. "A whirling, twirling, swirling—WHOA!"

Willow stumbled as a boy with lots of freckles zoomed down the slide and crashed right into her.

"Whoops!" cried the boy. "Sorry about that!"

"That's okay," Willow said. She felt a raindrop splash her cheek.

"Willow, this is Finn." Jeanie introduced Willow to the boy, who Willow thought looked nice.

The leaves rustled wildly on the trees. When a few more fat drops fell, Finn groaned.

"Oh man!" he said. "I really wish it wouldn't rain! Nico and I wanted to play capture the flag."

Willow looked up at the dark clouds and silently tapped the charm on her necklace.

Suddenly the air turned colder, and the raindrops seemed to freeze. It was snowing!

"This weather doesn't make any sense," said Jeanie. "I didn't bring a coat today!"

Willow shifted nervously. That wasn't right. She gave her necklace a worried tug.

A golden glow flashed. The sun burst through the clouds, and the whipping winds slowed to a gentle breeze.

"That was, uh, pretty weird," said Willow. She knew she sounded awkward.

Finn pulled a yellow flag from his back pocket.

"Who cares?" he said happily. "The game is back on! Wanna join?"

"Um, no thanks," said Willow, looking at Jeanie.

Finn shrugged and took off.

"Feel like going on the swings?" Willow asked Jeanie.

But Jeanie didn't answer. She just stared at Willow with her mouth wide open.

Chapter 7

WILLOW'S BIG SECRET

"You . . . you . . . you made the rain stop," sputtered Jeanie.

Willow stared down at her feet. Her cheeks were pink, and she had the same flushed look on her face that she'd had during the dodgeball mix-up.

"It went from raining to snowing to sunny in a few seconds. How is that even possible?" Jeanie asked.

When Willow didn't answer, Jeanie tapped her foot impatiently. She was not going to let this go until she got some answers.

Willow sighed. Then she glanced over her shoulder A few kids darted by playing capture the flag.

"Is there somewhere else we can talk?" Willow asked. "Somewhere quiet?"

Jeanie nodded and led Willow over to a bench under the oak tree. The low-hanging branches created a little private lair. It was the perfect spot for sharing secrets.

And Jeanie had a feeling Willow was hiding something.

Something big.

"So," said Jeanie. "What exactly is going on here?"

Willow took a deep breath and said, "The thing is . . . I'm sort of . . ." Willow trailed off. Jeanie couldn't hear her.

"What?" Jeanie asked.

Willow covered her mouth and mumbled something that sounded like "Imkerndurfah." Jeanie had the feeling that Willow was nervous.

"I can't hear you, Willow," Jeanie said gently. "But it's okay if you don't want to tell me."

"No, it's just that . . . I'm kind of . . . ," Willow said, turning to face Jeanie. "Well, I'm a genie!"

"Right." Jeanie nodded, but then stopped. "Wait—you're a *what*?" she asked.

"A genie," Willow repeated.

"Like . . . your name is actually Jeanie?" asked Jeanie.

"No, like I'm a real-live wish-granting genie," said Willow.

Jeanie didn't know what to say. She'd never believed in things like genies before. They weren't real. They couldn't be.

But something strange had definitely just happened.

"A genie," Jeanie repeated. "You're a genie, like, who does magic?"

"Yes," said Willow. "Well, sort of. I do grant wishes, but I haven't quite gotten the hang of it yet. That's why it snowed before it got sunny."

Jeanie stood up and looked around. "This is a joke, right? Where are the hidden cameras? Am I on TV?"

"No," said Willow. "This is not a joke. My mom is the director of the World Genie Association, and she expects me to be the best genie I can be. So when I passed the WGA entrance exam, we moved to Rivertown for my training."

Jeanie plopped back down on the bench. "So you're really a . . . genie. And you moved to Rivertown for your . . . genie training."

"Yep. My mom said Rivertown is the perfect place for me to practice granting wishes," Willow explained. "And if I collect enough skill badges, the WGA will make me a Master Genie! Can you believe it?"

Jeanie shook her head in a daze. She wasn't sure what to believe!

Chapter 8

WHAT-IFS

Willow held her breath. She could feel her heart beating fast. She needed Jeanie to not freak out.

The World Genie Association rules stated that genies-in-training were allowed to tell their secret to one person . . . and only one person. There was a section in the official genie manual all about it.

The rule was very clear. It said:

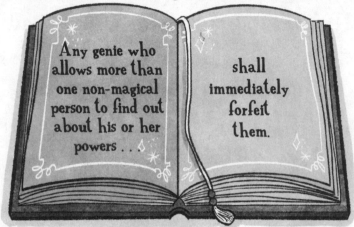

Any genie who allows more than one non-magical person to find out about his or her powers . . . shall immediately forfeit them.

That meant if anyone else found out about Willow, she'd never grant any more wishes, or earn any badges, or *ever* become a Master Genie!

Willow hadn't planned to tell anyone her secret so soon. But Jeanie was clever and kind and nice—the perfect person to trust.

Plus Jeanie was a really good student. Sometimes Willow had a hard time putting her skills to work. She could use all the help she could get practicing her wish-granting.

Still, Willow couldn't help thinking about all the what-ifs. What if Jeanie thought Willow was totally weird? What if she called Willow a liar? Or worst of all, what if Jeanie

told everyone Willow's big secret?

She hoped she'd made the right decision by choosing Jeanie.

Willow slid one hand behind her back and crossed her fingers. Then she slid the other hand back there and crossed those fingers too. She crossed her toes—and, for just a second, she even crossed her eyes. "So, what do you think?" she asked timidly.

From the look on Jeanie's face, Willow could tell she had a hundred questions on the tip of her tongue.

"So how does it work?" Jeanie asked. "Can you grant your own wishes?"

"No, that would be selfish," said Willow. "Genies grant wishes to help other people."

"What about a bad wish?" Jeanie asked. "Like if someone wants to rob a bank?"

"Nope. We're not allowed to do anything harmful," said Willow.

A long minute passed. "What if someone wishes for unlimited wishes?" Jeanie said suddenly.

Willow smiled. Jeanie had to be the most logical person she had ever met!

"I'm pretty sure that's against the rules," Willow said. "But remember, I've still got a lot to learn about being a genie."

"Well, I think it's . . ." Jeanie paused, and Willow's heart felt like it might explode.

"I think it's—awesome!" Jeanie whisper-shouted. "And I promise not to tell anyone. You can trust me."

Willow let out a huge sigh of relief. Her secret was safe.

Chapter 9

MAGIC CHARM

Jeanie couldn't stop thinking about Willow's secret.

She thought about it while Ms. Patel handed back their spelling tests.

She thought about it while she refilled Jelly Bean's water bottle.

She thought about it while she wrote her assignments down in her homework folder.

Jeanie had a million more questions. But she knew she couldn't let anyone overhear them. She had to wait until classroom 2B was packing up to go home.

Finally, Jeanie caught Willow's eye and motioned her over to the cubbies.

"I understand *why* you grant wishes," Jeanie began. "But *how* do you actually do it?"

Willow gave her a nervous smile. "I'm still trying to figure that out. I know that the person has to look me in the eye and say the words 'I wish.' And I know that they have to *really* mean it. I can only grant heartfelt wishes."

"That makes sense," said Jeanie thoughtfully.

"But I'm still trying to get the hang of wish granting," said Willow. "It's not as easy as it sounds."

"You can learn anything with practice," said Jeanie. She lowered her voice to a whisper. "But how do you know if your wish granting is working?"

Willow lifted the gold charm around her neck. "When a wish is about to be granted, my necklace glows."

Jeanie peered closely. It wasn't a teapot or an elephant's head after all. It was a magic lamp! The golden charm was even prettier than Jeanie had realized.

"Wow," Jeanie whispered.

"Girls, time to collect your backpacks, please," called Ms. Patel.

Jeanie hurried to zip her bag. But then she stopped suddenly.

"Wait!" she whispered to Willow. "Do you *live* in that lamp?"

Willow giggled. "No, silly, that's only in fairy tales. I live in a regular house. I bet it's a lot like yours."

As they headed for the door, the bells on Willow's bracelet tinkled cheerfully.

"Hey," said Jeanie, "speaking of houses, do you want to come over to mine this afternoon?"

Willow smiled.

Chapter 10

PRACTICE MAKES ALMOST PERFECT

Jeanie's bedroom looked exactly the way Willow had pictured it.

Her desk and closet were both as neat as a pin. Her bed was so perfectly made it looked like it belonged in a fancy hotel. And there was a *huge* bookshelf—organized alphabetically, of course.

Willow was so glad her mom had let her go over to Jeanie's for dinner.

She already couldn't wait for Jeanie to come see her room sometime! It was *much* different from Jeanie's— Willow had a crystal collection, art supplies, and snazzy clothes scattered all over the place.

Once the girls were alone, Jeanie got right down to business.

"So what happens now?" Jeanie asked Willow. "If I wished for the world's biggest ice cream sundae ... I could have it?"

"If you really want it, it's yours," said Willow.

"Nah," said Jeanie. "I don't feel like ice cream right now."

"Is there anything you *really* want?" Willow asked. She needed to practice to earn her Basic Gifting Badge. "What about a pony? Or a diamond tiara? Or a day off from school?"

Jeanie laughed and said, "Too messy. Too flashy. And do you know me at all yet?! I love school!"

That's when Willow got the perfect idea. She belly flopped onto Jeanie's bed, wriggling and flailing until both pillows were on the floor and the comforter was twisted into a ball. Then she looked up.

Just as she'd guessed, the mess *definitely* bothered Jeanie. She was scowling.

"Well, go ahead!" said Willow cheerfully.

For a moment Jeanie looked confused. Then she smiled.

She looked Willow straight in the eye and said, "I wish my bed would go back to the way it was."

Willow stood and gave her charm a gentle tap.

At first nothing happened.

Then the charm began to glow. Slowly the pillows floated up into the air. The comforter rippled and stretched until it was totally smooth. The pillows circled and drifted back down to their original spots on the bed.

Jeanie was shocked. "That's amazing!"

Willow laughed. "Oh, we can do better than that. Are you hungry for dinner?" Willow asked.

"Well, I really wish we could have pizza!" Jeanie answered.

Ding-dong!

"Is that what I think it is?" asked Jeanie. She raced to the window. A guy in a red-and-white uniform stood on the front porch with a steaming box that said GIO'S PIZZA.

Jeanie raced downstairs.

Willow smiled. She'd only been in town for a couple of days, and she'd already made a new friend . . . and not just any friend. A friend she could share her secret with.

Although Willow couldn't grant her own wishes, it was sort of like her wish had come true too!

LOOK FOR MORE

Jeanie & Genie

BOOKS AT YOUR FAVORITE STORE!